The
Boston Tea Party

A Level Three Reader

By Cynthia Klingel and Robert B. Noyed

The Child's World®

On the cover...
This drawing shows the Boston Tea Party.

Published by The Child's World®, Inc.
PO Box 326
Chanhassen, MN 55317-0326
800-599-READ
www.childsworld.com

Photo Credits
© Barney Burstein/CORBIS: 18
© CORBIS: cover, 21, 25
© Hulton Archives: 10, 13, 22, 26
© Kevin Fleming/CORBIS: 5
© Stock Montage: 6, 9, 14, 17, 29

Project Coordination: Editorial Directions, Inc.
Photo Research: Alice K. Flanagan

Library of Congress Cataloging-in-Publication Data
Klingel, Cynthia Fitterer.
The Boston Tea Party / by Cynthia Klingel and Robert B. Noyed.
    p. cm.
ISBN 1-56766-958-1 (library bound : alk. paper)
1. Boston Tea Party, 1773—Juvenile literature.
[1. Boston Tea Party, 1773. 2. United States—History—Revolution,
1775-1783—Causes.]   I. Noyed, Robert B. II. Title.
E215.7 .K53 2001
973.3'115—dc21
                            00-013174

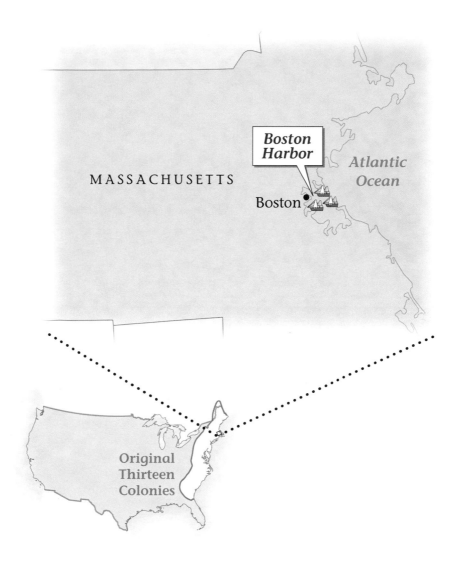

Do you know where the Boston Tea Party took place? Here is a map to help you find out.

The Boston Tea Party was an important **historic** event in early American history. It took place in Boston, Massachusetts, on December 16, 1773. It was one of the events that led to the Revolutionary War.

This is a copy of one of the three Boston Tea Party ships. →

In 1773, England controlled the thirteen American **colonies**. The people who lived in the colonies were called **colonists**. The colonists were growing unhappy under England's control. They wanted their freedom.

This drawing shows colonists in Boston reading a new British law.

The colonists had to pay taxes to England. They did not like giving England their money. The colonists did not think the taxes were fair.

Colonists in this drawing are burning British tax papers. →

[January, 1770]
[1773 (?)]

WILLIAM JACKSON,

an *IMPORTER*; at the

BRAZEN HEAD,

North Side of the TOWN-HOUSE,

and Opposite the Town-Pump, in

Corn-hill, BOSTON.

It is defired that the SONS and
DAUGHTERS of *LIBERTY*,
would not buy any one thing of
him, for in fo doing they will bring
Difgrace upon *themfelves*, and their
Pofterity, for *ever* and *ever*, AMEN.

The colonists bought many things from England. England charged taxes on these things. The colonists decided to stop buying goods that were taxed. One of these items was tea.

← Here you can see an American ad asking colonists not to buy English goods.

The colonists stopped buying tea from England. The tea began to pile up in English **warehouses**. Businesses were losing money. King George of England decided to lower the cost of tea so the colonists would buy it.

This is a painting of George III. He was the king of England at the time of the Boston Tea Party.

The colonists were angry. The king still made them pay the tea tax. The colonists did not like being controlled this way. They waited for ships carrying the tea to arrive in Boston Harbor.

This cartoon shows Americans attacking a tax collector.

When three ships arrived with tea, some colonists held special meetings. These colonists called themselves the Sons of Liberty. Samuel Adams and Paul Revere were leaders of the group. The Sons of Liberty wanted the ships to take the tea back to England.

This is a drawing of Paul Revere.

The ships were not allowed to return to England with the tea. They could not leave Boston Harbor until the tea was unloaded. To leave without unloading, the ships needed permission from the **governor** of Massachusetts.

Here you can see a drawing of ships being held in Boston Harbor.

The king had appointed the governor of Massachusetts. The governor's name was Thomas Hutchinson. Hutchinson did not support the colonists. He ordered the ships to stay until the tea was unloaded.

This illustration shows colonists fighting against British rule. →

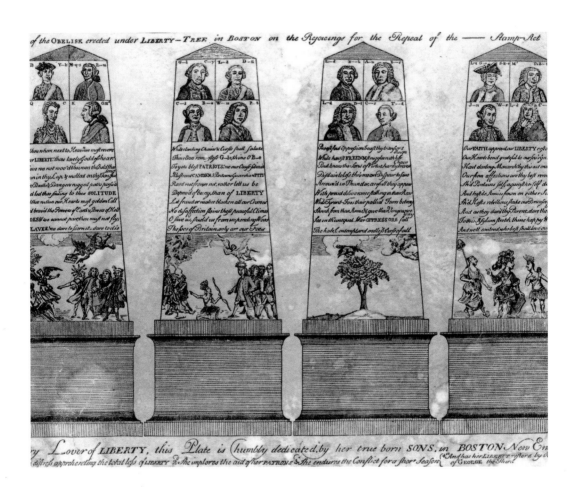

The Sons of Liberty continued to meet secretly. They tried very hard to solve the problem. They were getting nowhere. Then they came up with a plan.

← Here you can see a political drawing of the Sons of Liberty.

After dark on December 16, a group of men and boys marched through town. They were dressed as Native Americans so they would not be recognized. They went to the harbor and boarded the three ships.

This drawing shows the night of the Boston Tea Party. →

They smashed open the chests of tea. They threw the tea into the water. The group worked quickly and quietly. They were careful not to damage anything else on the ships.

Here you can see colonists smashing open chests of tea.

By morning, the harbor was quiet. There was no tea left on the ships. The tea **merchants** would not be paid. The king would not receive his tax. The colonists had shown England they wanted freedom. Before long, the Revolutionary War would begin.

This drawing shows a battle in Lexington, Massachusetts. It was the first battle of the Revolutionary War.

Glossary

colonies (KOL-uh-neez)
Colonies are lands ruled by a
faraway country.

colonists (KOL-uh-nists)
Colonists are people who live in
a colony.

governor (GUV-urn-er)
A governor is someone who
controls an area using laws.

historic (hih-STOR-ik)
When something is historic, it is
an important part of the past.

merchants (MER-chents)
Merchants are people who
sell goods.

warehouses (WAYR-how-sez)
Warehouses are big buildings
used for storing goods.

Index

To Find Out More

Books

Hemphill, Kris, and John Martin. *A Secret Party in Boston Harbor.* New York: Silver Moon Press, 1998.

Knight, James E. *Boston Tea Party: Rebellion in the Colonies.* Mahwah, N.J.: Troll Associates, 1998.

Stein, R. Conrad. *The Story of the Boston Tea Party.* Chicago: Children's Press, 1984.

Web Sites

Boston Tea Party Ship and Museum
http://www.bostonteapartyship.com
Describes the museum in Boston and features online activities for kids.

Liberty!: High Tea in Boston Harbor
http://www.pbs.org/ktca/liberty/chronicle/episode1.html
For a fictional newspaper article describing the Boston Tea Party.

Samuel Adams, Art in the U.S. Capitol
http://www.aoc.gov/art/nshpages/adams.htm
For information about one of the organizers of the Boston Tea Party.

Note to Parents and Educators

Welcome to The Wonders of Reading™! These books provide text at three different levels for beginning readers to practice and strengthen their reading skills. In addition, the use of nonfiction text gives readers the valuable opportunity to *read to learn*, not just to learn to read.

These leveled readers allow children to choose books at their level of reading confidence and performance. Level One books offer beginning readers simple language, word choice, and sentence structure as well as a word list. Level Two books feature slightly more difficult vocabulary, longer sentences, and longer total text. In the back of each Level Two book are an index and a list of books and Web sites for finding out more information. Level Three books continue to extend word choice and length of text. In the back of each Level Three book are a glossary, an index, and a list of books and Web sites for further research.

State and national standards in reading and language arts emphasize using nonfiction at all levels of reading development. The Wonders of Reading™ books fill the historical void in nonfiction for primary grade readers with the additional benefit of a leveled text.

About the Authors

Cynthia Klingel has worked as a high school English teacher and an elementary teacher. She is currently the curriculum director for a Minnesota school district. Writing children's books is another way for her to continue her passion for sharing the written word with children. Cynthia is a frequent visitor to the children's section of bookstores and enjoys spending time with her many friends, family, and two daughters.

Robert Noyed started his career as a newspaper reporter. Since then, he has worked in communications and public relations for more than fourteen years for a Minnesota school district. He enjoys writing books for children and finds that it brings a different feeling of challenge and accomplishment from other writing projects. He is an avid reader who also enjoys music, theater, traveling, and spending time with his wife, son, and daughter.